Track_ ... the Snow

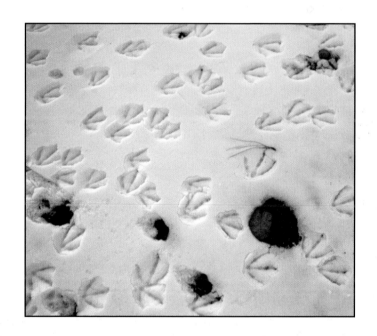

Written by Ratu Mataira

Rigby

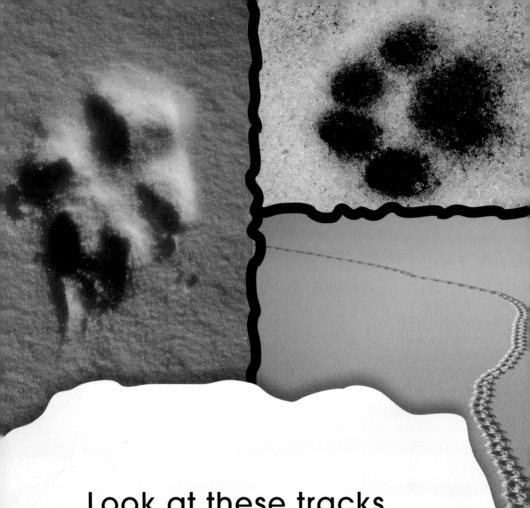

Look at these tracks.
These tracks are
in the snow.

They were made by animals
that live in the snow.

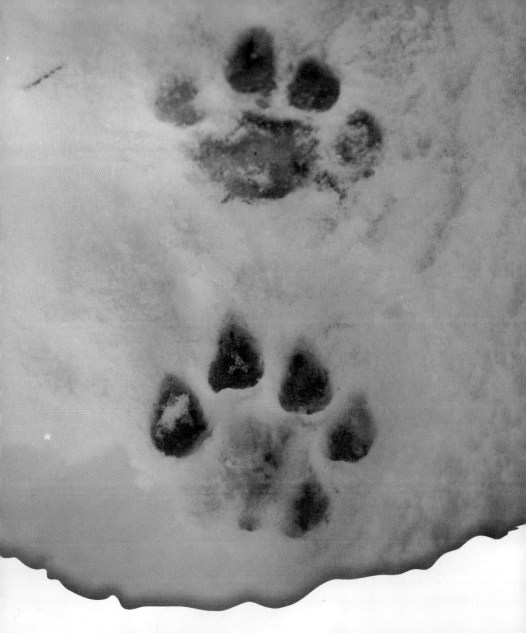

Look at these tracks.
What has been here?

mountain lion

It was this big cat.
It made these tracks
in the snow.

Look at these tracks.
What has been here?

It was this rabbit.
It ran over the snow
to get away from the cat.
It made these tracks
in the snow.

Look at these tracks.
One track is big and
one track is small.
What has been here?

raccoon

It was this raccoon.
It came down from
a tree to look for food.

Look at these tracks.
What has been here?

It was this penguin.
It went over the snow
on its stomach and
made these tracks.

Look at these tracks.
What has been here?

It was this fox.
It is looking for a place
to sleep.

Look at the fox now.
It can't make tracks
in the snow
when it is sleeping!

Look at all these
tracks in the snow.
These tracks were made
by people.

Index

Guide Notes

Title: Tracks in the Snow
Stage: Early (3) – Blue

Genre: Nonfiction
Approach: Guided Reading
Processes: Thinking Critically, Exploring Language, Processing Information
Written and Visual Focus: Photographs (static images), Index, Labels
Word Count: 175

THINKING CRITICALLY
(sample questions)

- Look at the front cover and the title. Ask the children what they know about animals that make tracks in the snow.
- Look at the title and read it to the children.
- Focus the children's attention on the index. Ask: "What are you going to find out about in this book?"
- If you want to find out about tracks made by a penguin, which pages would you look on?
- If you want to find out about tracks made by people, which page would you look on?
- Look at pages 10 and 11. Why do you think a penguin would go over the snow on its stomach?
- Look at pages 14 and 15. What other tracks do you think people could leave in the snow?

EXPLORING LANGUAGE

Terminology
Title, cover, photographs, author, photographers

Vocabulary
Interest words: tracks, snow, mountain lion, raccoon, penguin, fox, stomach
High-frequency words: what, been
Positional words: in, over, down, on

Print Conventions
Capital letter for sentence beginnings, periods, exclamation mark, question marks